TOMB ROBBERS

Written by Ross Montgomery
Illustrated by Luke Ashforth

RISING ★ STARS

ISBN: 9781398325555

Text © Ross Montgomery
Illustrations, design and layout © Hodder and Stoughton Ltd
First published in 2022 by Hodder & Stoughton Limited (for its Rising Stars imprint, part of the Hodder Education Group),
An Hachette UK Company
Carmelite House, 50 Victoria Embankment, London EC4Y 0DZ
www.risingstars-uk.com

Impression number 10 9 8 7 6 5 4 3 2 1
Year 2026 2025 2024 2023 2022

Author: Ross Montgomery
Series Editor: Tony Bradman
Commissioning Editor: Hamish Baxter
Illustrator: Luke Ashforth/Bright International Group
Educational Reviewer: Helen Marron
Design concept: Julie Joubinaux
Page layouts: Rocket Design (East Anglia) Ltd
Editor: Amy Tyrer

With thanks to the schools that took part in the development of *Reading Planet* KS2, including: Ancaster CE Primary School, Ancaster; Downsway Primary School, Reading; Ferry Lane Primary School, London; Foxborough Primary School, Slough; Griffin Park Primary School, Blackburn; St Barnabas CE First & Middle School, Pershore; Tranmoor Primary School, Doncaster; and Wilton CE Primary School, Wilton.

A catalogue record for this title is available from the British Library.

Printed in the UK.

Orders: Please contact Hachette UK Distribution, Hely Hutchinson Centre, Milton Road, Didcot, Oxfordshire, OX11 7HH.
Telephone: (44) 01235 400555. Email: primary@hachette.co.uk.

MIX
Paper from
responsible sources
FSC™ C104740
FSC
www.fsc.org

Contents

CHAPTER 1:
THEBES, ANCIENT EGYPT, 1315 BC

Seth peered out of his bedroom window. It was the dead of night. The streets of Thebes were silent as a tomb. Even the insects were quiet now.

He prayed that no one would hear him climb out of the window.

As quiet as a mouse, he slid down the wall and landed on the dust in his bare feet. The midnight air was freezing cold, but the ground was still warm from the desert sun. He looked around the empty courtyard. In the day, his house would be filled with noise: his brothers and sisters playing, his mother feeding chickens. Now, there was no one except Seth and the stars.

He hoped it would stay that way.

He slipped out of the courtyard, moving quickly through the dark city streets to the banks of the River Nile. He knew exactly where he was going: back to the marketplace. The place where he had spent all afternoon, playing with his friends. Where he had stashed his prized marble collection for safekeeping.

Seth cursed himself. How in the name of Osiris had he left them there?

Seth had worked for years on his marble collection, winning game after game until he had won the most beautiful set in all of Thebes. That afternoon, after his friends grew bored of Seth winning yet another game, they had dared him to steal some fruit from one of the market sellers.

He'd hidden his precious marbles inside an old broken pot in an alleyway – then been chased all the way home by an angry fruit seller. He wished he had never done it in the first place – but at least he'd had a lucky escape. Until he woke in the middle of the night and realised that his marbles were still where he'd left them.

He came to the riverbank. It was pitch black, but Seth could hear the water quietly licking at the path beside him. The market was only a short walk away now – if he was quick, he'd be back home and safe in his bed in minutes.

He paced along the bank, his eyes fixed on the stars above him. It seemed like they were all out tonight – Seth almost felt as if they were watching him. Each one of those stars belonged to the gods. Seth could spot the star that belonged to the god Osiris, and the goddesses Isis and Nut ... and there, brightest of all, was the star known as *Sopdet*. The star of the dog-headed god, Anubis.

Seth shivered. Egypt had many gods, but Anubis was the god of death. It was his job to make sure that people passed safely into the afterlife when they died: that was why his picture was painted on all the tombs around Thebes. There was no greater crime than breaking into someone's tomb and stealing the belongings they'd been buried with – people said that if you did that, then the god Anubis would punish you in the afterlife.

People still robbed tombs, though – especially in the Valley of the Kings, where the great pharaohs who ruled Egypt were buried with all of their riches.

These tombs, just a few miles outside the city limits, were filled with a fortune in gold, jewellery and precious oils: that was why guards patrolled the valley each night, protecting them from tomb robbers.

All the pharaohs were buried there – even the boy-king, Tutankhamun.

Seth kept his eyes fixed to the sky, walking faster now. Tutankhamun wasn't one of the most famous or well-known pharaohs. His rule had lasted barely ten years ... but even so, Seth had always liked the sound of the boy-king. His father, the pharaoh Akhenaten, had tried to stop people worshipping many of the gods: he had closed temples and even destroyed monuments.

It had made Akhenaten very unpopular – so when Tutankhamun became pharaoh, he made sure to reopen the temples and rebuild the monuments. The boy-king had stood up to his father – Seth liked that. He wished that he could do that himself sometimes.

Of course, people still thought that Tutankhamun had been cursed by his father's mistakes. They said it was the reason he had been unwell throughout his short life, and why he had died so young. There were even rumours that his final resting place in the Valley of the Kings was cursed, and that anyone who dared to break into it would become cursed themselves ...

Seth shivered again. He didn't need to keep scaring himself like this. The streets of Thebes were dangerous enough as it was, filled with thieves and robbers. He just needed to find his marbles and get home, fast.

Every second that he lost was a second when his father might find out that he'd left the house.

He finally reached the market. During the day it was the busiest part of the city, but now it was a silent square littered with old fruit and camel dung. He raced to the alleyway where he had hidden his stash – and sure enough, there was the broken pot. He reached inside it, heart pounding, praying that his marbles would still be there ...

He breathed a sigh of relief as his hands closed around the familiar cloth pouch. They were here – they hadn't been stolen after all. Seth lifted out the bag and opened the string to reveal his hidden treasures. The marbles twinkled in the starlight.

"This is my lucky day," he whispered.

A hand suddenly clamped around his mouth.
Seth dropped his marbles and tried to scream,
but it was no use – the man's hands were huge
and rough, his arms as thick and strong as tree
trunks.

"Here! I've got one!" the man hissed.

He spun Seth around – and Seth saw that there
was another man, standing in the darkness at
the end of the alleyway.

Seth couldn't see his face ... but his eyes
gleamed like the eyes of a cobra. He looked Seth
up and down, as if
measuring him,
and nodded
quickly.

"He will do – now come! We've lost enough time as it is."

Without a moment's pause, the huge man swung Seth up into his arms as easily as if he were a bag of apples. Then, quick as a flash, the men carried him out of the market.

Seth's mind was racing. Who were these men? Where were they taking him? He tried to scream again, but it was no use – the man's enormous hands were clamped over his mouth. There was no way to get free from his strong grip.

Soon, they were pacing down the road that led out into the desert. There were no more houses out here beyond the city limits – now, no one would hear even if Seth did manage to cry for help.

Seth panicked. Were these men trying to rob him? Did they think his marbles were a bag of money? He had to make them understand before it was too late. He bit down on the fingers covering his mouth, making the huge man howl with pain and tear his hand away. Seth took his chance.

"Please – you must let me go!" he begged. "I have nothing for you to steal!"

The two men stopped, surprised, then the one with cobra eyes began to laugh.

"Listen to him, Bek! He thinks we are common robbers!" He leaned close. "We're not stealing from *you*, street-rat – it's *you* who is going to help *us* do the stealing!"

Seth had no idea what this man was talking about. How was he going to help them steal something? There was nothing out here in the desert: all the houses were back in the city. The only place out here was ...

Seth's whole body filled with horror. The Valley of the Kings. The final resting place of the pharaohs. *That* was where the men were taking him.

The man with cobra eyes leaned even closer.

"That's right, street-rat," he whispered. "It really is your lucky day. Tonight, you're going to help us break into the tomb of the boy-king Tutankhamun!"

CHAPTER 2:
THE VALLEY OF THE KINGS

Seth stared at the two men in disbelief. This couldn't be true – *surely* these two weren't planning to break into the sacred tomb of Tutankhamun? Tomb robbing was one of the worst crimes there was – that's why the Valley of the Kings was so heavily guarded, and all the temples were sealed up so that no one could ever break into them. There was no way that these men would get inside one of them – let alone with Seth's help. *And what about the curse?*

The huge man named Bek held up his bitten hand. "Look, Ottah – the rat nearly took my fingers off!" He snarled in Seth's face. "I say we throw him from the top of the valley!"

The man named Ottah shook his head.

"Don't be an idiot, Bek. We need the boy. Now come on. We don't have much time!"

With that, Ottah turned and strode along the desert road. Seth fought and tried to scream for all he was worth, but it was hopeless. Bek clamped a hand back over Seth's mouth and followed Ottah like an obedient dog. Bek might be the stronger of the two, but Ottah was clearly in charge.

"I still don't get why we're going to all this trouble," Bek grumbled. "We should be robbing the tombs belonging to Thutmose or Akhenaten. There'll be much more inside them that's worth stealing!"

Seth frowned – Bek had a point. Tucked away in a dark corner of the valley, the tomb of Tutankhamun was much smaller than the other tombs.

After all, no one was expecting the boy-king to die at such a young age. It meant they only had 70 days to build his tomb, while they normally took years to build.

"That's exactly your problem, Bek," Ottah spat. "You don't get *anything!* We're robbing Tutankhamun's tomb *because* it's small. The guards are all busy protecting the grand tombs at the other end of the valley – the guards we haven't paid off, at least. No one thinks there's anything valuable inside Tutankhamun's tomb!"

His eyes flashed greedily in the dark.

"But I know the truth. I was one of the workers who helped construct it – and I saw what they built beside the burial chamber. A treasury, Bek! Mark my words – that tiny tomb is going to be stuffed with more riches that you could possibly imagine. Gold! Jewels! And it's all there for the taking. By the time dawn comes, we'll be rich!" He glanced around. "Now, silence! You know the punishment if we're caught."

Ottah began slithering down a steep slope, his feet dragging in the dirt. There were no trees here, no grass: the land was dry and dead. Seth felt himself fill with dread – he knew what it meant. They were already entering the Valley of the Kings.

He knew what would happen if they were caught, too. If the criminals were lucky, sometimes they were simply flogged or beaten on the soles of the feet. Sometimes though, they had their hands or feet cut off as punishment. But worst of all, if the crime was *really* serious … it meant execution. Death.

Seth began to panic. He had no idea why these men were getting him involved, but no one would believe him if he said that he'd been captured and forced to break into the tomb against his will. What if the fruit seller from the market came forward and said that Seth had stolen some food from him that very day? His fate was already sealed. He would be caught and punished, along with Ottah and Bek – he might even be put to death himself.

There was only one hope for him now – one chance for survival.

He had to break free from Bek's grip and escape across the desert. It was deadly at night, filled with snakes and scorpions ... but it was better than what was waiting for him here.

Seth might be small, but he was still fast enough to outrun two men in the dark. He struggled for all he was worth, kicking and punching at Bek's shoulders, screaming against his rough hand.

But he was too late. With a great heave, Bek threw him off his shoulder and dumped him on the dusty ground. Seth was completely winded, all the breath knocked out of him – he couldn't cry out now, even if he wanted to.

He looked around, panting. Up ahead stood a sheer rock face, stretching to the sky like a thundercloud. At its bottom was a carved stone staircase, leading down to a dark entrance. It didn't look much like the final resting place of a pharaoh. In fact, it looked more like a cave. But Seth knew where he was. It was the entrance to Tutankhamun's tomb.

And the tomb wasn't the only thing that was waiting for them ...

"Finally!" a voice grunted. "What took you so long?"

Seth gazed around in horror. Before him stood a dozen men – each one as broad, mean and tough as Bek. They surrounded him on every side, cutting off any hope of escape.

And then Seth understood the truth. There was no way he could get away from these horrible men now. The guards wouldn't hear him if he screamed. And even if they did hear him, he was doomed.

He was trapped.

CHAPTER 3:
THE PHARAOH'S TOMB

The silence didn't last for long. One of the men grabbed Seth from the dust and dragged him to his feet, sizing him up like a piece of meat.

"*This* is what you went to the city for, Ottah?" he growled. "You've brought back some street-kid to help us?"

Ottah shot him a glance. "I didn't have much of a choice, did I, Ebo? Not after the mess your men have made of the break in!"

Ebo snarled. "*Mess?* We've been working on that tomb for seven hours, and we still have nothing! We're almost out of time – the sun will be up soon!"

Ottah turned to Seth and smiled. "That's how our street-rat friend is going to help us ..."

Ebo shook his head. "You're out of your mind, bringing him into this. Once the job's done, that boy's going to tell every person in Thebes!"

Seth suddenly found his courage. Ebo was right – he couldn't let himself be dragged into such a terrible crime. He pushed free from Ebo's grip and glared at Ottah.

"He's right – I will!" he cried. "I'll never help you break inside that tomb. You should all be ashamed of yourselves!"

The men all fell silent. Ottah froze, fixing Seth with those gleaming cobra eyes. Seth felt his knees turn to water. Ottah suddenly strode forwards and grabbed Seth, pulling him close.

"Listen carefully, Boy. You're going to do every last thing that I tell you ... or I'll make you pay for it, ten times over. One more refusal like that – any attempt to escape or alert the guards – and I'll make sure you never leave the Valley of the Kings alive. And if you dare to tell anyone about us, then it will be the last thing you ever do. Punishment by the guards will be *nothing* compared to what I'll do to you. Understand?"

Seth nodded in fear – he believed every word that Ottah said. No wonder all these men did whatever he told them.

With that, Ottah spun Seth around and flung him towards the stone staircase.

"Now, get inside," said Ottah. "We don't have much time!"

Seth stumbled down the staircase, his mind reeling. He still had no idea why he was here. How on earth was he supposed to help these men break inside a tomb? The doors were all sealed with stone. But as Seth got closer, he realised that the cave entrance was covered with a dark sheet. Ottah threw it open, revealing a hole knocked through the tomb entrance. The men had already broken in, covering up their work so that the guards wouldn't see. Seth gasped. They had smashed right through a picture of Anubis himself.

"Get inside," Ottah hissed.

Seth was filled with horror. He wasn't really going to crawl through the hole, was he? Anubis was the god of the dead – the protector of tombs. If Seth stepped inside that tomb, he'd spend all his time in the afterlife being punished. And what about the curse?

"N–no ," he whispered, his voice shaking. "I can't ..."

Before he could say any more, Bek strode forward and shoved him through the hole. Seth tumbled inside the tomb, landing painfully on the dusty floor.

"I thought I'd give him a little nudge!" Bek laughed.

Seth looked up, heart pounding. He was in a small, dark room, pitch black and freezing cold. The room was empty, except for the rubble on the floor.

Ottah crawled through the hole behind him, followed by Ebo and Bek – someone outside passed through a flaming torch and covered the entrance again so that the guards wouldn't catch sight of its flickering glow.

The dark room lit up around them. Seth was surprised: this didn't look like the final resting place of a grand pharaoh. It was little more than a corridor – small and badly made. The plaster on the walls had been slapped on, rather than carefully smoothed and painted. The builders had clearly rushed to finish it. Seth suddenly felt a wave of pity for Tutankhamun – what a poor, sad, lonely place this was.

"Keep going, Rat!" said Ottah, shoving him forwards.

Seth did as he was told – there was no way out for him now. The corridor led to another sealed entrance, which Ebo's men had also broken through. There was a hole at the top, just big enough to crawl inside. Seth quickly clambered through before Bek could shove him again.

The room inside was barely bigger than the corridor – but it wasn't empty. It was filled with all kinds of objects: jars of oil, withered flowers, sandals, trumpets, metal plates. Seth knew what they were doing here. These were the things that Tutankhamun had loved most in life, gathered together so he could take them with him to the afterlife.

In one corner was a chariot wheel, a memory of how much the boy-king loved racing. There, resting on a far wall, was even his old walking stick – the one he had used because of his limp.

But everything had been thrown to the floor. Some of the precious objects had even been smashed.

Seth gasped in horror. The robbers had turned it all over to search for the gold they'd been promised. They'd thrown the objects to one side like they were nothing. But they *weren't* nothing – these were Tutankhamun's most prized possessions. Surely, *surely* the curse would follow them now? Right in front of Seth's horrified eyes, Ebo turned his head and spat on the floor.

"Pah!" he snarled. "Seven hours of work, and all we have to show for it is a room of useless junk!"

"I *told* you," said Ottah. "The gold is all inside the burial chamber!"

He held out the torch to the far wall. At the end of the room was another blocked-up entrance. On either side of the entrance stood two black and gold statues, holding swords to protect it from intruders. It was the entrance to the burial chamber: the final resting place of Tutankhamun's body. Surely these men weren't going to break inside *there*, too? But sure enough, at the bottom of the entrance, another hole had been smashed through. This one was much smaller than the others, though.

"See?" said Ebo. "That's the biggest hole we could make – there's no way any of us will be able to squeeze inside it!"

Ottah shrugged. "It's too big for one of *us*, maybe ... but it's the perfect size for a worthless street-rat."

Seth felt his stomach drop. He understood the truth. *That* was why they had brought him here – they were going to make him crawl inside the burial chamber and steal Tutankhamun's treasure for them.

"Well? What are you waiting for, Boy?" said Ottah, his face flickering in the flames of the torch. "Get inside."

CHAPTER 4:
THE BURIAL CHAMBER

Seth stared at Ottah in horror. He couldn't believe what he was hearing – stealing from a person's burial chamber was the single worst thing a person could do. This tomb was meant to be a sacred place.

"N–no!" Seth cried. "I won't do it!"

He threw himself at the men, kicking and fighting for all he was worth to try to escape ... but it was absolutely hopeless. With a roar of impatience, Bek grabbed him and forced him to the floor again.

"You heard what he said," he roared. "Now, get inside and find us that gold!"

Bek was too strong – kicking and screaming, Seth was forced through the hole and into the burial chamber.

He scrambled to his feet in terror, pressing his back against the stone wall. Before him was deepest, darkest black. The air tasted of age and dust. He could hear something scuttling around him. Was the floor covered in snakes and scorpions? Or was it even Anubis himself, the dog-headed god of the afterlife, already come to take his terrible revenge on Seth?

A hand suddenly appeared through the hole, holding a flaming torch.

"Take it!" Ottah hissed. "What do you see?"

Seth took the torch with shaking hands and held it up, desperate for any light. He looked around ... and gasped.

This room wasn't like the others, covered in bare rough plaster. The walls here were coated in shimmering gold. It was a beautiful sight – and what's more, the golden walls were painted with incredible scenes. They showed Tutankhamun's journey from this world into the afterlife. There was a picture of his mummified body being pulled on a sledge towards his final resting place. There was even a picture of him being welcomed into the underworld by Anubis himself!

And there, in the middle of the chamber, was the shrine. The great golden box where Tutankhamun's body was stored.

Seth trembled. The shrine was enormous; it was so close that Seth could reach out and touch it.

On the side were more pictures of Anubis. The eyes of the dog-headed god gleamed in the torchlight, as if watching him.

"Answer me, Boy!" Ottah snapped. "What do you see? Is there another room beside you?"

Seth turned and saw that Ottah was right. There was another chamber leading from this one, almost as big as the first. "Y–yes. There is."

"That's the treasury! Did I not tell you?" came Ottah's voice, gloating at the others. "Look inside, Boy – what do you see?"

Seth filled with dread. Looking inside the treasury meant leaving the wall – it meant walking right past the shrine itself. He felt certain that the painting of Anubis was watching his every move now, growing angrier and angrier with him ...

But he had no choice. The faster he gave these men what they wanted, the faster he could get out of here. He forced himself to leave the wall and walk across the burial chamber, his feet shaking with every step, his eyes fixed on the pitch-black chamber ahead that was slowly glowing into light ...

Seth gasped again. Everything Ottah had said was true. The treasury was filled with gold, jewels, statues, priceless works of art and sparkling boxes made of precious metals. Seth had never seen so many beautiful things in his entire life.

"It … it's here," said Seth. "The treasury."

He heard Bek and Ebo cry out for joy outside.

"I knew it!" said Ottah. "Now, quick, Boy – take everything you can and pass it through the hole!"

Finally, Seth found what little bravery he had left. There was nothing the men could do to him while he was in here – for the very first time, he was in control. He turned back to the hole in the door, glaring at Ottah.

"No," he said. "These treasures don't belong to you – these belong to the boy-king. You can threaten me all you like, but I will not help you!"

Ottah's eyes fixed on him through the hole, and a smile crept on to his lips.

"Then we'll brick you up inside it," he whispered.

Seth's heart lurched. That couldn't be true – the men would never do a thing like that, would they?

"You heard me, Rat," said Ottah. "If you don't do what we say, I will get Bek to block this hole with the biggest, heaviest stone he can find. You'll spend the rest of your days alone inside this tomb, with nothing but the dead for company. Is that what you want?"

Seth gazed around the tomb, shaking from head to foot with fear. The thought of spending days inside this pitch-dark room with no food or water ... it was unthinkable. Surely Ottah was just trying to frighten him? But once again, he gazed into those cobra eyes gleaming through the hole in the doorway ... and he knew that Ottah was capable of anything.

"You've got one final chance, Boy," Ottah hissed. "Hand us the gold."

Seth closed his eyes. Ottah was right – this was his final chance. So, he did the only thing left that he could do: he prayed.

Tutankhamun – Anubis. Forgive me for what I'm about to do. Have mercy on me!

With shaking hands, he picked up a golden statue and carried it over to the hole in the doorway. He passed it through – and heard gasps of amazement as the men gazed upon the riches.

"What did I tell you?" said Ottah. "More, Rat!"

Working as fast as he could, Seth grabbed treasure after treasure and carried them back to the hole in the entrance, stuffing each one through to Ottah's greedy hands. The men fought and bickered over the riches, passing them back in a line to the men waiting outside. Seth felt sick to his stomach – there was no way that he would ever escape the curse now. Surely any moment the punishment would arrive and ...

He suddenly heard a sound behind him – a footstep. He swung around, gasping with fear. But there was no one there – it must have been something falling over in the treasury. He *was* still alone in here, wasn't he?

"Hurry up, Rat!" Ottah cried. "Or do you want a beating for your troubles as well?"

Seth swallowed and did as he was told. He ran back to the treasury, emptying box after box. But as he worked, the sense that he wasn't alone grew thicker and faster – he felt as if something was building, like a terrible moment would come at any second. He had to finish this and get out of here as fast as he …

Then it came. A scream.

Seth spun round in horror, his heart raging like a storm in his chest. The scream had come from the other side of the burial chamber door – a scream of absolute terror. It was followed by another, and another – it was Ottah and Ebo and Bek. Seth had never heard grown men scream like that before.

"G–get away! Run!"

Seth stood, frozen to the spot. There were more shouts now, more cries of fear from outside. The men were all running away. Seth realised at once what must be happening. The guards had come – they'd been caught! Was this the end for Seth? Was he ever going to see his family again?

Or was it even worse than that – had the statues guarding the burial chamber come to life to take terrible revenge on the robbers? Had the curse of Tutankhamun's tomb finally appeared – and was it now coming for Seth?

The silence that followed the screams was the worst sound of all. The tomb was still and unmoving around him – Seth's heart pounded, and his breath heaved in and out.

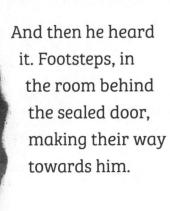

And then he heard it. Footsteps, in the room behind the sealed door, making their way towards him.

Seth backed away from the door in horror, his whole body shaking as he held out the torch. There was something moving through the hole at the bottom of the door – something slowly making its way into the burial chamber towards him.

Seth froze. It was a hand – the hand of a young boy.

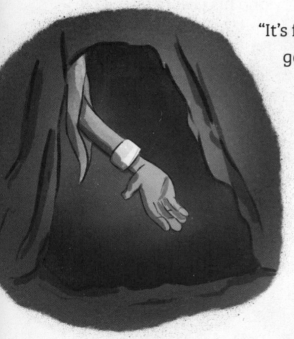

"It's fine – they are gone. You can come out now."

CHAPTER 5:
THE SUN RISES

Seth stood, staring at the hand in shock. He wasn't imagining it – there really was a young boy's hand sticking through the hole of the burial chamber door.

"Come," the boy said again. "It's safe, I promise. I'll pull you through."

Seth had no idea what was going on. He hadn't seen any other boy with the tomb robbers outside – if there had been one, there'd have been no need for Seth. What was a boy doing out here in the middle of the night?

"Quick!" said the boy. "Before the guards come!"

Seth blinked. "Are they not here now?"

"No, but they will be soon," said the boy. "Come on, take my hand."

Seth didn't need any more persuading. He took one final look at the shrine, and then scampered across the burial chamber and grabbed the boy's hand. It was colder than he'd expected. It must have been the night air. He dropped the torch and allowed himself be dragged back out of the burial chamber.

Without the torch to see by, the room on the other side was pitch black. Seth couldn't even make out the face of the boy who had saved him. But he could see that the robbers had left in a hurry. Ottah, Bek and Ebo had even thrown some of the treasure to one side, keen to leave as fast as they could.

"What happened?" asked Seth.

"They had a bit of a scare," said the boy, a smile in his voice. "I have a feeling that Ottah won't be breaking into any more tombs."

Seth gazed at the room in pity. It was still covered in Tutankhamun's damaged treasures.

"We can't leave it like this," he said, filled with guilt. "If the god Anubis finds out what I have done ..."

The boy laughed. Seth looked at the boy but still couldn't see his face.

"Do not worry about Anubis – he knows who is guilty and who is innocent. The priests will repair the holes in the walls so that no one can break inside again."

Seth was confused. Who was this boy? He spoke like he knew Anubis as a friend. Seth still couldn't make out his face in the darkness ... but before he could ask any questions, the boy took his hand and led him carefully out the room.

"Now, come – you cannot stay here any longer. Let me show you out."

He led Seth carefully back to the tomb's entrance. Seth slithered out into the cold night air and gazed at the valley around him, glowing in the first rays of sunlight. He never thought he'd be so glad to see outside again. The air had never tasted so good. He felt as if he had just left the land of the dead.

"It is almost sunrise," said the boy. "You should go home, before the next shift of guards arrives."

The boy was right. The sky to the east was slowly changing colour – daybreak would be here within the hour. Seth was going to have to run as fast as possible if he wanted to be home before his parents woke up. He had a feeling that his father might have a few words for him – but after everything he had gone through tonight, Seth felt that dealing with an angry father was nothing. He wasn't worried about his marbles, either: they could stay where he had dropped them in the alleyway. Storing treasure led to nothing but trouble.

"Run – as fast as you can," said the boy, a note of sadness in his voice. "And do not look back."

The boy's voice was suddenly commanding – Seth found himself doing exactly as he was told, racing across the dusty valley floor away from the tomb.

It was only after he had run a short distance that he realised he hadn't had the chance to thank this mysterious boy for all his help. After all, he had saved Seth from certain death – he had made sure that the guards hadn't found him, and had given him help when he needed it most. But Seth didn't know his name – he didn't even know what he looked like.

He turned around.

"Thank you!" he called out. "For–"

Seth trailed off. In the rising sun, he could finally see the boy who had saved him from the dark tomb. He was not much older than Seth himself. He stood proudly, one hand resting on a walking stick beside him. His eyes were dusted with dark patches of black make-up … and on top of his head, shining in the sun, was a golden headdress.

Seth was speechless. He watched as the boy-king Tutankhamun gave him a final nod and limped back down the staircase to the tomb's entrance. Then, as if the stone doorway was made of nothing more than desert air, he stepped right through the wall and disappeared inside.

Chat about the book

1 Read Chapter 1. Why did Seth leave his home in the middle of the night?

2 When Seth entered the treasury he found 'priceless works of art'. What does 'priceless' mean?

3 Go to page 9. Why did Seth like that the boy-king had stood up to his father? What does this suggest to us about Seth and his father?

4 On page 15, it says, 'The man with cobra eyes leaned even closer. "That's right, street-rat," he whispered. "It really is your lucky day."' How does the author make the man appear threatening?

5 Why do you think the boy at the end of the story helped Seth?

6 Go to page 24. Read the sentence at the end of the chapter. Why did the author end the chapter in this way?

7 Read pages 32 and 33. What does the first small, dark room tell us about Tutankhamun, and why do you think it is important for the story?

8 *Tomb Robbers* is a ghost story. Do you enjoy ghost stories? How do they make you feel?